Father Christmas and the Cats in Magic Boots

By, Morris Ferrari

Help Wanted: Our Earth Needs Help Right Now!

In a snug little cottage, tucked away in the Village of the Cats in Magic Boots, deep in the Northern Enchanted Forest near Father Christmas's home in Lapland, lived a clever and kind-hearted cat called Eugene.

Eugene was the clever leader of the Cats in Magic Boots, a little village full of amazing cats. Each cat had a special pair of magic boots that helped them jump really far—almost like flying— faster than you could blink!

Eugene had made the Magic Boots himself. He was a brilliant inventor who loved creating wonderful new things to help his furry friends.

These boots weren't just magical — they were cosy, waterproof, and always a perfect fit, no matter who wore them.

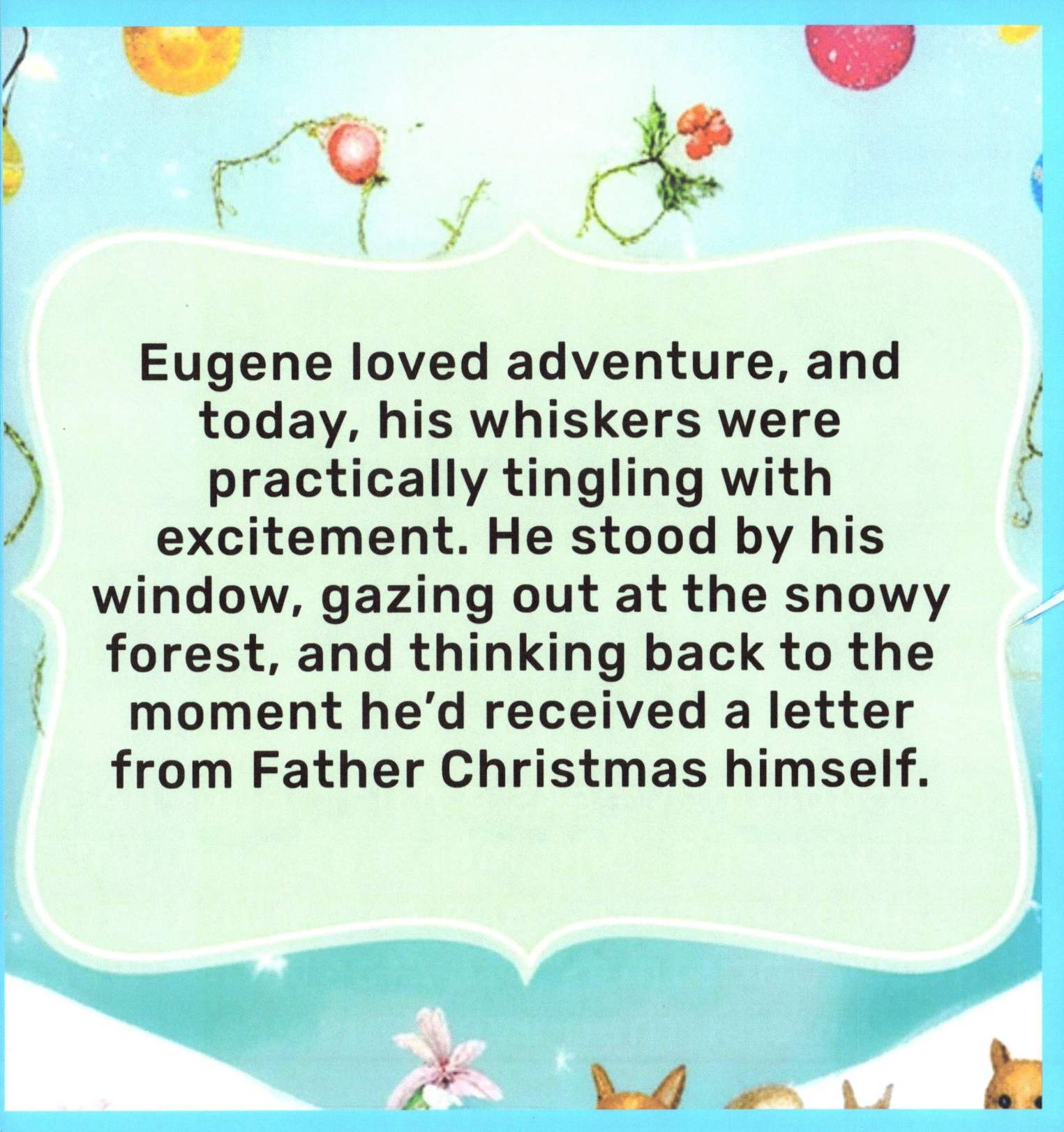

Eugene loved adventure, and today, his whiskers were practically tingling with excitement. He stood by his window, gazing out at the snowy forest, and thinking back to the moment he'd received a letter from Father Christmas himself.

A couple of weeks earlier, Eugene's fairy friend, Glimmer, had brought some big news. She told him that Father Christmas's toy factories were busier than ever this year.

So Eugene sat down, wrote a letter to Father Christmas, and offered their help. To his great delight, Santa replied with a resounding "Yes!"

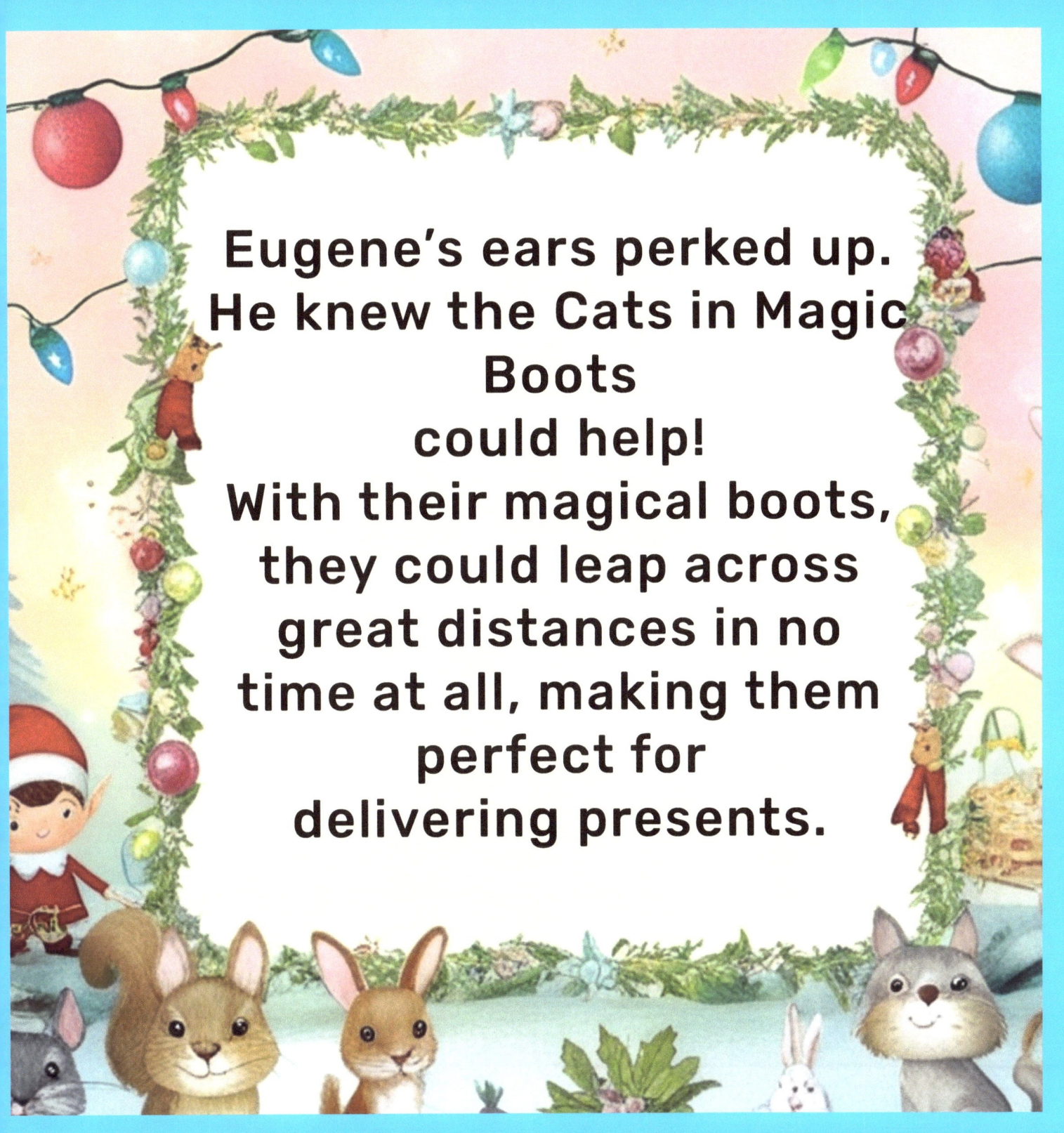

Eugene's ears perked up.
He knew the Cats in Magic Boots
could help!
With their magical boots,
they could leap across
great distances in no
time at all, making them
perfect for
delivering presents.

Eugene had dreamed of this day for years, and now, at last, it had come true!

The big move to Lapland was arranged, and the cats were set to begin their journey on a Friday evening, just as the sun dipped behind the trees.

Eugene remembered an old Cat in Boots—Chats Bottés in French—called Napoleon. He was known for being super speedy, really smart, and always looking fancy!

A new generation of talking cats in boots has arrived - led by Napoleon, the brave protectors of Mother Earth!

A long time ago, a wise cat named Napoleon led the Cats in Boots. He showed everyone that being smart, kind, and caring for nature and animals could make the world a better place.The cats put down their swords and chose to use honesty and wisdom instead. Many years later, a clever cat named Eugene became their new leader. He made the Magic Boots even better and taught the cats that the greatest magic of all is kindness, bravery, and working together.

To welcome the Cats in Magic Boots, the elves had even built a brand-new village filled with snug little cottages, all ready for their arrival.

The Journey North

As the evening stars began to twinkle, Eugene and the Cats in Magic Boots set off on their journey to Lapland.

The air was icy, but the cats' magical boots kept them warm and dry. With each leap, they soared twenty miles closer to their destination, bounding through the snowy night like fluffy shooting stars.

When they finally arrived, Eugene gathered his fellow cats for a hearty meal and a moment of gratitude. They had made it!

The next morning, Eugene could barely contain his excitement. Not only was he about to meet Father Christmas and Mamma Christmas, but he was also going to visit the famous Toy Factories—something he'd dreamed of since he was a kitten.

**Meeting Father Christmas
and Mamma Christmas**

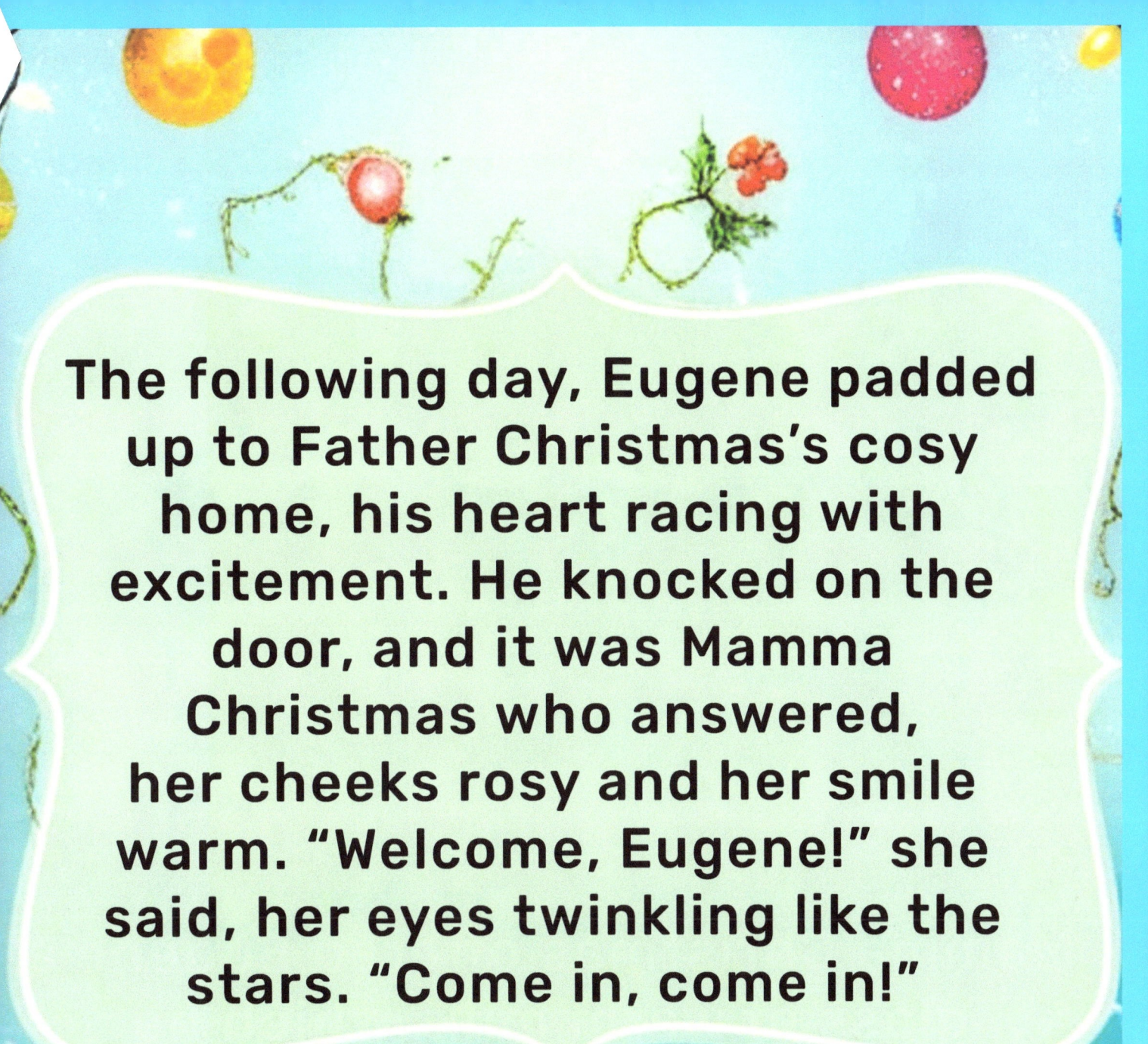

The following day, Eugene padded up to Father Christmas's cosy home, his heart racing with excitement. He knocked on the door, and it was Mamma Christmas who answered, her cheeks rosy and her smile warm. "Welcome, Eugene!" she said, her eyes twinkling like the stars. "Come in, come in!"

Mamma Christmas offered Eugene a glass of warm milk, which he happily accepted. As they sipped their drinks,

Eugene asked the question that had been on his mind. "Father Christmas, after all these years, why do you need extra help now?"

Father Christmas sighed, his cheerful smile fading just a little. "The world is changing, Eugene," he said.

"The forests, rivers, and oceans are being harmed by pollution. My elves need the magic of nature to create toys."

Father Christmas continued. "Without healthy forests, their magic doesn't work as well."

"That's why we need extra help this year. The magic of Christmas depends on the world staying green and beautiful."

Father Christmas showed Eugene a lovely picture of a kind elf teacher with her little students in the Enchanted World.

Eugene's ears drooped slightly. "I understand," he said. "We'll do everything we can to help—and we'll even stay to protect the forests if you need us!"

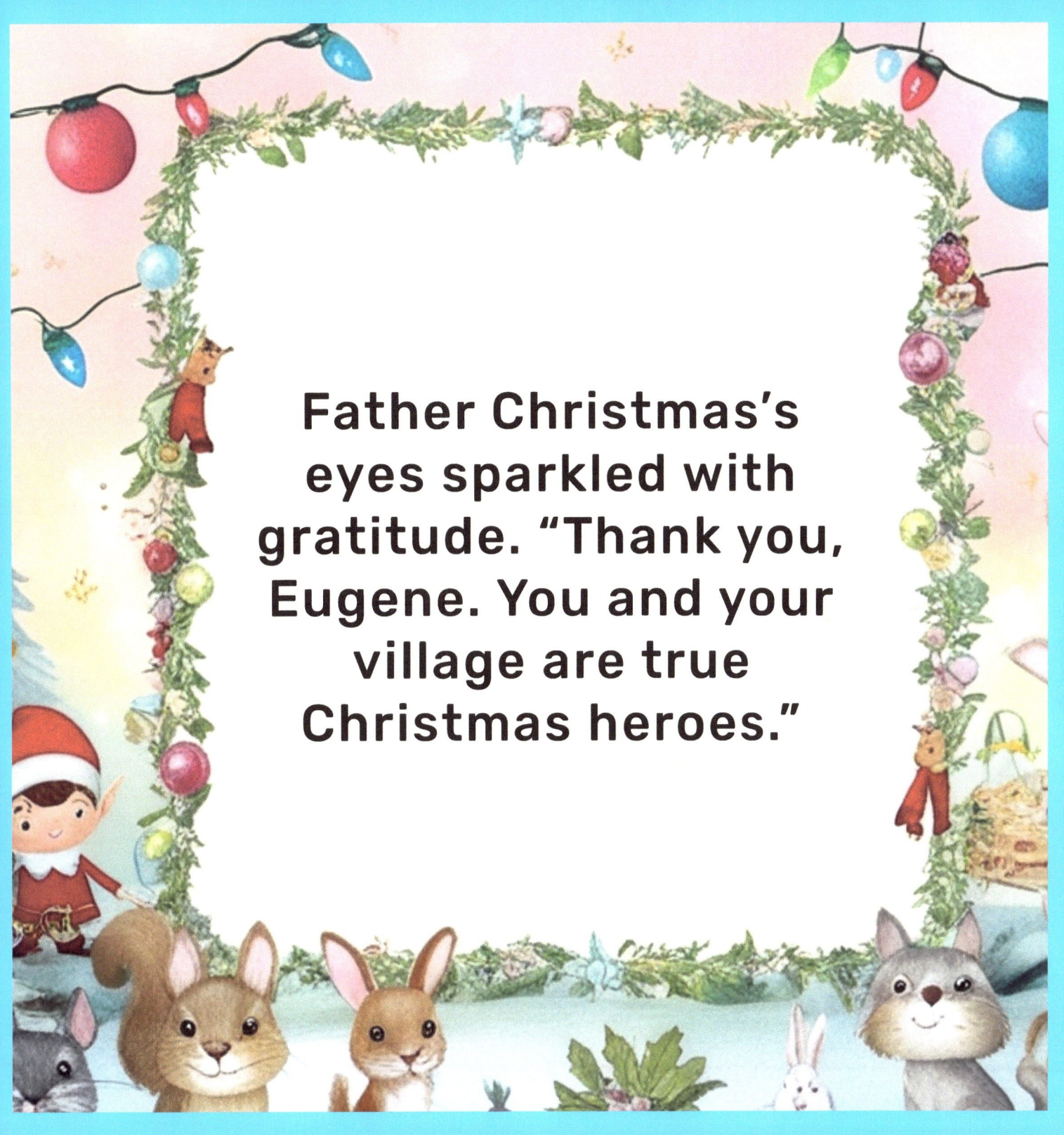

Father Christmas's eyes sparkled with gratitude. "Thank you, Eugene. You and your village are true Christmas heroes."

Preparing for the Big Day

After a delicious lunch with Father Christmas and Mamma Christmas, Eugene visited the Toy Factories.

What a sight it was!
Millions of toys were being made,
each one carefully wrapped and
labelled with a child's name.

There were millions of presents waiting to be delivered

The days that followed were filled with hard work and preparation. The Cats in Magic Boots practised their leaps and learned their delivery routes.

Christmas Eve – The Greatest Presents Delivery

Meanwhile, the elves worked on building new super sleighs. These sleighs were unlike anything Eugene had ever seen—sleek, silent, and powered by giant, magical batteries instead of reindeer.

They could carry millions of presents and glide just above the ground without a sound.

On Christmas Eve, the Cats in Magic Boots would team up with the elves to deliver presents to children all over the world. It was going to be the most magical night ever.

At last, Christmas Eve arrived!
The super sleighs were packed to
the brim with brightly wrapped
presents.

The Cats in Magic Boots, dressed in festive red scarves, stood ready to spring into action.

Father Christmas climbed into his traditional sleigh, still led by his trusty reindeer, and gave the signal. "Ho, ho, ho! Let's go!"

Each cat carried two sacks of presents—one in each paw—and with a single bound, they landed softly on rooftops or outside doors. Quiet as snowflakes, they delivered gifts to children around the world.

With their special trackers, the cats found each house with ease, dropped off the presents, and darted back to the sleighs for more.

They worked tirelessly, leaping, landing, and delivering until every single present was safely in place.

Thanks to the incredible teamwork of the elves, the Cats in Magic Boots, and, of course, Father Christmas and Mamma Christmas, the night was a resounding success.

It was the greatest
present delivery the
world had ever seen —
a true Christmas miracle!

A Christmas Celebration

When the last present was delivered, everyone returned to Lapland for a grand celebration. The elves, the cats, Father Christmas, and Mamma Christmas gathered in a big, cosy hall filled with twinkling lights and the smell of delicious food.

There was laughter, music, and stories of their adventures. Eugene sat by the fire, his heart full of joy. He knew this was a Christmas he and his village would never forget.

www.ingramcontent.com/pod-product-compliance
Lightning Source LLC
Chambersburg PA
CBHW041538240626
47164CB00002B/50